Toto in Rome

BIDDY STREVENS

A first taste of Italy for young children

LITTLE, BROWN

Boston · Toronto · London

Illustrations and text copyright © 1991 by Bridget Strevens Romer

First published in Great Britain in 1991
by Little, Brown and Company, (UK) Ltd
Beacon House, 30 North End Road, London W14 0SH

Designed by Janet James and Bet Ayer
Typeset by DP Photosetting, Aylesbury, Bucks
Printed and bound in Belgium
by Proost,
Turnhout

ISBN 0-316-88885-0

A CIP catalogue record for this
book is available from
the British Library

"What a lovely boy you are!" says Signora Rossi. "You look just like your *mamma*
did when she was little."

"Please can I go and look at the fountain?" Toto asks.

"Careful you don't drop your *gelato*!" says Toto's father.

"Don't wander too far off, will you!" says Toto's mother.

"Do your parents boss *you* about all the time?" Toto asks a nearby cat. But the cat has his eye on a fat pigeon and is thinking about something quite different.

"Hey, look out!" warns Toto as the cat loses its balance and falls into the water with a huge SPLASH.

"Toto to the rescue!" he cries and plunges in.

"Help! *Aiuto*!" Signora Rossi shouts and pulls Toto out by his trouser legs.

"Don't let go!" cries Toto to the cat.

"MiaOW, miaOW!" the cat complains.

"*Mamma mia!* What a state you're in, both of you! You'd better come round the corner to my shop and dry off a little."

"Lucca! Don't just sit there, get some towels," says Signora Rossi. Toto and the cat drip all over the shop.

"Lucca put that newspaper down and do what I say," insists Signora Rossi.

But Lucca carries on reading: "Pippo the puppeteer cannot work without his cat. Ginger, white and black with unmistakable red and green collar. A generous reward offered for his recovery."

It doesn't take long for Toto to dry off.

"Thank you. This is delicious *pizza*," he says from under his towel.

"In Italian you say *grazie!*" Signora Rossi tells him.

"Come here kitty," whispers Lucca, "see what I've got for you."

"Ooops!" says Lucca as the mouse slips from his fingers and runs for its life!
What a commotion!

"A mouse in my shop! *Non e possibile!*" screams Signora Rossi as cakes and
biscuits and *pasta* are sent flying.

"I think I'd better get back to my parents," says Toto, but no-one takes any notice.

"You'll never guess what just happened!" Toto says excitedly. 'Not now, Toto, we're concentrating," his parents reply.

"Come on now, Toto. Quickly. Jump on the bus!" says his mother. "There are lots of places to visit in a beautiful old city like Rome."

But they are not the only ones going on a sightseeing tour.

Toto and his parents wander around some very old buildings.
 "Look at that!" exclaims Toto's father, taking a photograph.
 "Well, look at this! The cat with the lovely collar!" whispers Toto.
 "How did you get here? Where are your parents?"

"I wonder where you live? Do you understand me?"

"PRRRRR" replies the cat, surveying the view of Rome.

"What's keeping you, Toto!" his father calls. "Stop lagging behind, there's lots to see. Come down and join us at once!"

"I'm coming," Toto calls. He and his little friend make their way past a stone lion and up yet more steps.

"It looks nice and cool up there," says Toto.

"Shhh! I don't think cats are welcome in museums. If anyone sees you, pretend you're a statue."

"How very true to life!" comment some tourists behind their cameras.

"Now let's play hide and seek," says Toto. "You hide and I'll count to five in Italian, like Signora Rossi taught me. *Uno, due, tre, quattro, cinque* . . . ."
With his eyes shut Toto doesn't notice Lucca sneaking up on them.

"Hey, come back, that's not your cat!"

"It's not yours either!" shouts Lucca.

"I know, but he's my friend, not yours. Come back!"
Off roars Lucca on his moped. "*Ciao!* Bye!"

Just then, as Toto is beginning to think he'll never see his new friend again, along comes Signora Rossi in her delivery van.

"Let's go, *andiamo!*" she says. "*Presto, presto*, hurry up and get in. I've worked out what Lucca is up to, and I know where he's going!"

"Did you know that you rescued a very special cat?" asks Signora Rossi.

"Oh yes, I know he's special," says Toto proudly.

"But did you know that he works for Pippo the puppeteer? Look, here's his picture in the newspaper." Signora Rossi talks non-stop as they rumble along in the van.

"BRRRRR" roars Lucca's moped.

"GRRRRR" growls the cat in the basket.

In the puppeteer's tent, a happy reunion is taking place.

"*Il mio gatto*, my cat! A miracle!" says old Pippo the puppeteer. "*Grazie, mille grazie!* How can I thank you for returning him safely?"

"It wasn't easy, I can tell you. But I did read that there was a reward . . . ."

At the word "reward" the cat hisses and spits at Lucca.

"Now that's very puzzling!" says Pippo.

"Ah, I see. You prefer this little boy . . . ."

"I'm quite big now," interrupts Toto, breathlessly.

"This little boy saved your cat from drowning, Signor Pippo," pants Signora Rossi. "I saw it with my own eyes. And as for you, Lucca, all you think of is rewards! *I'll* give you a reward! You're going to spend the rest of the day clearing up the shop!"

"*Per favore*, Signora, please. I'm so happy to get my cat back that I'll give *everybody* a reward," says Signor Pippo.

"Please, *per favore*, someone listen to *me*!" asks Toto. "What about my parents? Can we go back to collect them from the museum?"

"Phew! What a crush!" says Toto's father as they squeeze into
the back of Signora Rossi's van with Pippo, Toto and the cat.
  "I can't make myself any smaller!" squeaks Toto's mother.
  "Neither can I," says Toto, "I'm big now, don't forget."
Off they go, through the market square.

"*È pronto il pranzo*. Lunch is ready," announces the chef.

"What mountains of *maccheroni*, what torrents of *tortellini*, what seas of *spaghetti*!" sings Pippo.

"What a reward! *Mille grazie!*"

dolciumi

dollchóomee

forchetta

forkéttah

pianta della citta

peeánta délla chittáh

francobollo

frankobólo

cartolina

cartoeléenah

pasta

pástah

tortellini

tortelléenee

cottello

cottélloe

pizza

péetzah